THE HAUNTED HISTORY OF CHICAGO, ILLINOIS

BY RACHEL SEIGEL

Cover image: The Chicago Water Tower was designed by architect William W. Boyington. Boyington also designed many other important buildings in the city of Chicago during the mid-1800s.

abdobooks.com

Published by Abdo Publishing, a division of ABDO, PO Box 398166, Minneapolis, Minnesota 55439. Copyright © 2024 by Abdo Consulting Group, Inc. International copyrights reserved in all countries. No part of this book may be reproduced in any form without written permission from the publisher. Core Library™ is a trademark and logo of Abdo Publishing.

Printed in the United States of America, North Mankato, Minnesota.
102023
012024

Cover Photo: Shutterstock Images
Interior Photos: Felix Lipov/Shutterstock Images, 4–5, 43; Bettmann/Getty Images, 8; Chicago History Museum/Archive Photos/Getty Images, 10–11, 14; PHAS/Universal Images Group/Getty Images, 16; Lario Tus/Shutterstock Images, 18–19, 45; Shutterstock Images, 20; Wikimedia Commons, 22–23; Pamela Brick/Shutterstock Images, 26–27; Paul Walsh/AP Images, 28; Chronicle/Alamy, 30; Red Line Editorial, 33, 39; Joe Klamar/AFP/Getty Images, 34–35; James Berry/Alamy, 36

Editors: Priscilla An and Marie Pearson
Series Designer: Ryan Gale

Library of Congress Control Number: 2023939636

Publisher's Cataloging-in-Publication Data
Names: Seigel, Rachel, author.
Title: The haunted history of Chicago, Illinois / by Rachel Seigel
Description: Minneapolis, Minnesota: Abdo Publishing, 2024 | Series: Haunted history of the United States | Includes online resources and index.
Identifiers: ISBN 9781098292515 (lib. bdg.) | ISBN 9798384910459 (ebook)
Subjects: LCSH: Haunted places--United States--Juvenile literature. | History--Juvenile literature. | Ghosts--United States--Juvenile literature. | Chicago (Ill.)--History--Juvenile literature.
Classification: DDC 133.109--dc23

CONTENTS

CONGRESS HO

CONGRESS PLAZA HOTEL

man named John started working as a security guard at Chicago's Congress Plaza Hotel in the 1990s. One day, he received a call about a little boy running around and making noise on the twelfth floor. When he went to investigate, at first he didn't see anything. Then he spotted a little boy. The boy was standing at the far end of the hotel's hallway wearing worn-out clothes. John pointed at the boy and told him he wasn't supposed be up there. The boy looked at him, grinned, and slowly disappeared where he was standing.

The Congress Plaza Hotel opened in 1893. It is a historic location in the city.

John said he saw the boy a couple more times at the hotel, and even once in his own home.

Some people believe the boy might be the ghost of six-year-old Karel Langer. In 1939, Adele Langer, a Jewish refugee from Czechoslovakia, came to the United States with her two sons. They were fleeing the Nazis, which was a political party in Germany that wanted to harm Jewish people and others because of their race, religion, or other factors. Adele became desperate as she looked for a job and waited for her husband to come. After weeks passed, Adele couldn't handle it anymore. She threw her sons out a hotel window before jumping herself. Strangely, Karel's body disappeared before getting to the morgue. Some people believe he is still at the hotel.

CHICAGO'S MOST HAUNTED SPOT

People say that the Congress Plaza Hotel is the most haunted hotel in Chicago and the most haunted place in all of Illinois. The hotel is also known as the Home of Presidents because it has hosted many US presidents. The famous gangster Al Capone supposedly played cards in the hotel every Friday night in the 1920s.

There are many rooms in the hotel that

THE GHOST OF AL CAPONE

Of all the ghosts rumored to haunt the Congress Plaza Hotel, the most famous is Al Capone. Stories say he ran his headquarters in the hotel and used it to smuggle drugs and guns. Many guests have reported seeing a large man who looks like Al Capone wearing a suit and walking along the eighth-floor corridors in the north tower.

people think are haunted, but the most haunted room
is believed to be room 441. More people have called
the front desk to complain about that room than any
other room in the hotel. Guests have reported a figure
standing near the foot of the bed who wakes them up
with kicking and banging noises. Guests have also said
they've seen doors opening and closing on their own.

HISTORICAL SIGNIFICANCE

There have been many stories of hauntings in Chicago.
Parapsychologists suggest that people who died
suddenly or violently may be tied to the place of their
death. They think this explains some hauntings.

In the 1920s, Chicago had a reputation for gangs, dishonesty, and chaos. This was especially true during the period known as the Prohibition era, which started in 1920 when the sale of alcohol was banned. Many Chicago locations associated with the famous gangster Al Capone are said to be haunted, including the now destroyed Lexington Hotel and the site of the Saint Valentine's Day Massacre. These locations and the many other haunted places in Chicago are all part of Chicago's rich history and have their own unique stories to tell.

FURTHER EVIDENCE

Chapter One talks about the haunted history of the Congress Plaza Hotel. What is the main point of this chapter? Read the article from the website below. Does the article support the point made in the chapter? Does it offer any new evidence?

THE HAUNTED CONGRESS PLAZA HOTEL

abdocorelibrary.com/haunted-chicago-illinois

HAUNTED LANDMARKS

The Chicago Water Tower is one of the oldest buildings in Chicago's history. Built in 1869, it's the second-oldest water tower in the United States. It pumped water from Lake Michigan, and the Chicago Fire Department used it to put out fires. However, there wasn't enough water stored in the tower to put out the Great Chicago Fire of 1871. That fire destroyed much of the city. The water tower was the only surviving building in the burn area.

The Chicago Water Tower was not damaged in the Great Chicago Fire of 1871 in part because it is made of little to no wood.

GREAT CHICAGO FIRE OF 1871

A German firefighter named Frank Trautman helped save the Chicago Water Tower from burning down. During the Great Chicago Fire, Trautman covered the building in woolen blankets and thrown-away canvas sails that were soaked in lake water. This protected the water tower from flying cinders and flaming garbage. After the fire, the water tower was seen as a symbol of determination for the city as people began to rebuild.

There are many stories about the Chicago Water Tower being haunted. One popular story is about the ghost of a man who was operating the water pumps during the fire. When he realized the fire couldn't be contained, he went up to the top and hanged himself. Since then, many people reported seeing the shadow of a man in one of the top windows of the tower. The police have been asked to investigate ghost sightings many times over the years, but they've never found anyone or anything to explain the sightings.

RED LION PUB

The Red Lion Pub is considered one of Chicago's most haunted bars because of its violent history. The original bar was built in 1882 and was called Dirty Dan's Western Saloon. It was surrounded by farms and countryside. As the city developed in the 1920s and 1930s, the pub became a popular hangout for Al Capone and other mobsters. In the 1940s, the bar resembled an Old West Saloon, and respectable people stayed away. The bar is also located across the street from the supposedly haunted Biograph Theater.

The pub is believed to be haunted by many ghosts. One of the ghosts is a female spirit who lives in a stall in the women's bathroom. Whenever she is around, the air turns unusually cold, and people smell a strong scent of lavender. The spirit is known to knock plates out of servers' hands, lock the door when someone is inside the bathroom stall, and shriek wildly. There are also reports of several male spirits at the pub, one of whom is believed to be the former owner, Dirty Dan Danforth.

COOK COUNTY JAIL

In the 1800s, the old Cook County Jail stood at the corner of West Illinois Street and Dearborn Street. A larger jail was built to the southwest in 1871, but due to overcrowding in the new jail, some prisoners were also held in the old jail. At the time, Chicago allowed executions, and some prisoners were hanged in the building.

The old jail already had a reputation for being haunted. Prisoners reported hearing hammers pounding late at night after workers had left. Guards also claimed to see chairs moving on their own at night and papers disappearing and then reappearing later in strange locations. There were also reports of ghosts, including the ghost of a young prisoner named Peter Neidermeier, who was hanged in 1904.

Neidermeier and his friends were leaders of the Car Barn Bandits gang. They were responsible for several robberies and the deaths of eight men. Before his execution, Neidermeier promised to return and make everyone involved with his death sorry for hanging him.

Soon after Neidermeier's hanging, the paranormal activity

PERSPECTIVES

THE PRISONER AT OLD COOK COUNTY JAIL

In 1906, a reporter entered the jail and spoke with the guards and prisoners to find out more about the hauntings. One prisoner the reporter spoke to shared his experience:

I know there are ghosts here. A few nights ago, I woke up and there was a dim light over my cot. I felt a hand placed on my head, and then the light went out. I jumped up, but my cell door was locked. No living man could possibly have been in my cell. You ask me, this place is haunted; I know it's haunted.

Many hangings took place at Cook County Jail.

got worse, and many people believed Neidermeier had come back to haunt them. At midnight the night before the prison's forty-fifth hanging, in June 1906, everyone in the jail was frightened by a disturbing noise. The guards ran to the execution room. They found the trapdoor of the hanging platform had fallen and the rope was cut. There was no explanation for the noise or the cut rope. The old jail was eventually torn down, and a fire station now stands in its place. However, people still report hauntings in the fire station, including the sound of a moaning ghost.

STRAIGHT TO THE
SOURCE

The prisoners and the guards at the old Cook County Jail reported many strange happenings. The following excerpt is from an article published in the *Chicago Tribune* newspaper in 1906:

> *Before Peter Neidermeier, the car barn bandit was carried to his death . . . in the corridor of the old jail he cursed all who had anything to do with his execution saying just before he was hung: You can't kill me, you scoundrels, I will come back, and when I do come you will be sorry for what you have done. . . .*
>
> *The old timers at the jail laugh at the idea, but at the same time admit that when midnight comes, they hesitate to enter the [execution] room, where, if the stories told are true, the most weird noises are heard.*

Source: "Haunted Police Stations of Chicago." *Chicagology*, n.d., chicagology.com. Accessed 31 Mar. 2023.

BACK IT UP

The author of this passage is using evidence to support a point. Write a paragraph describing the point the author is making. Then write down two or three pieces of evidence the author uses to make the point.

HAUNTED CEMETERIES

Chicago has several cemeteries that people believe to be haunted. One is Resurrection Cemetery, which is reportedly the home of one of Chicago's most famous ghosts, Resurrection Mary. She gets her name from the cemetery, where she is thought to be buried.

According to legend, sometime in the late 1920s, Mary was walking home from the Oh Henry Ballroom. It was raining, and as she walked, she was hit and killed by a car. Since then, many people have spotted a young

Resurrection Mary is often seen between the cemetery and the ballroom she danced at the night that she died.

woman dressed in a white gown hitchhiking down Archer Avenue in search of a ride. Some drivers have said they picked Mary up, but she vanished before they got to their destination.

Jerry Paulus was the first person to report seeing Mary, in 1939. After dancing with her all night at a dance hall, which was formerly the Oh Henry Ballroom, he offered to drive her home. She told him she lived on the South Side of Chicago but asked him to take her to Archer Avenue, in the opposite direction. He dropped her off in front of Resurrection Cemetery before she disappeared. Wanting to know more about the woman, Jerry went to the address Mary had given him earlier.

Her mother answered the door, and she told him that Mary had died years ago. That's when Jerry realized he must have been dancing with a ghost.

BACHELOR'S GROVE CEMETERY

Bachelor's Grove Cemetery is believed to be one of the most haunted cemeteries in the United States. More than 100 hauntings and paranormal encounters have been reported there. Since the 1960s, visitors have talked about spooky and strange experiences. During the

Prohibition era in the 1920s and 1930s, gangsters supposedly dumped bodies and hid their illegal weapons in the pond behind the cemetery. Many people have reported seeing red or blue lights blinking, glowing brightly, and weaving around the tombstones both day and night. They believe that the lights are the spirits of those men.

Since the late 1960s, visitors have reported seeing a house while driving past or walking in the cemetery.

The first records of Bachelor's Grove becoming a cemetery date back to 1864.

However, there are no houses in that area. Many people also reported seeing a soft light burning in the window. When people see the house and try to get closer, it starts to shrink and eventually disappears.

One of the most well-known stories about Bachelor's Grove Cemetery is about the White Lady, also called the Woman in White. She appeared in a photograph taken by paranormal investigators exploring the cemetery in 1979. She was described as wearing a hooded robe and carrying a baby. Other sightings describe her as wearing a white dress and moving through the cemetery looking for something. In 1991, she was caught on camera again by a member of the local Ghost Research Society group. Now it is one of the most famous ghost photographs in the world.

STRAIGHT TO THE
SOURCE

There have been many variations on the legend of the disappearing house. Peter Crapia, a ghost guide and researcher at Bachelor's Grove Cemetery & Settlement Research Center, discusses these variations:

> *The most common description is a small white two-story house with a porch. . . . But upon follow-up visits it is nowhere to be found. Another common report is witnessing a house out near the cemetery but later the witness hears that no house is known to exist in the area. . . . In other accounts witnesses experience a transparent-like image of the house. . . . Occasionally witnesses report the house as "shrinking" when they approach it and it eventually disappears from their view.*

Source: Pete Crapia. "Paranormal History: Disappearing House." *Bachelor's Grove Cemetery & Settlement Research Center*, 26 Jan. 2023, bachelorsgrove.com. Accessed 2 May 2023.

CONSIDER YOUR AUDIENCE

Adapt this passage for a different audience, such as your principal or friends. Write a blog post conveying this same information for the new audience. How does your post differ from the original text and why?

Victory Gardens
BIOGRA
TODAY
2433
STARTS OCTOBER 26
Fade
Olagón
December 8-9

HAUNTED THEATERS

T heaters are some other supposedly haunted locations in Chicago The Victory Gardens Biograph Theater, formerly called the Biograph Theater, was built in 1914 in Chicago's Lincoln Park neighborhood. This is where Federal Bureau of Investigation (FBI) agents shot and killed the famous bank robber John Dillinger in 1934.

The night Dillinger was killed, he went to watch a movie with his girlfriend Polly Hamilton and her roommate Anne Sage. FBI agents set

The interior of the Victory Gardens Biograph Theater was completely remodeled in the early 2000s. Reports of ghost sightings have continued since then.

up a trap for him with Sage's help. Sage promised to wear a red dress so that the agents could recognize Dillinger. When Dillinger and the women came out of the theater, the FBI was waiting. The agents told him to surrender, but instead, Dillinger ran toward the alley, so they shot him.

People have said the theater is haunted by Dillinger's ghost, who continues to relive his death. Beginning around the first renovation of the theater in 1970, people started seeing the ghostly figure of a man leaving the theater, running toward the alley, falling and hitting the pavement, and then disappearing. Some people also believe that the inside of the theater is haunted. They report cold spots and uneasy feelings.

IROQUOIS THEATRE FIRE

When the Iroquois Theatre was built in 1903, it was supposed to be fireproof. But a city fire captain noticed many problems with the theater. There was too much wood trim, no fire alarm, and no sprinkler system. There was also only a single staircase when there should have been two,

WAS IT REALLY DILLINGER?

Some people believe that John Dillinger didn't die outside the Biograph Theater. Instead, they think he changed his appearance and got away. One theory is that the person who died was Jimmy Lawrence, a gangster who looked similar to Dillinger. Some medical evidence suggests the man who died was a different height and appearance than Dillinger. Also, Dillinger's father said the body wasn't his son's.

Magazines and newspapers published illustrations of the rush for the exits during the fire.

one for each balcony. The fire captain reported this

to the fire warden, who was responsible for fire safety in

the building. The fire warden knew he would lose his job

if he told the owners, so he stayed silent.

During the second act of an afternoon performance

on December 30, 1903, an electric lamp broke and

created a spark that caused a stage curtain to catch fire.

The stagehands tried to put out the fire, but the flames

were too high up on the stage for them to reach. They also tried to lower a special fire-resistant curtain, but it got stuck. When the audience realized that the fire couldn't be contained, they ran toward the exit doors. However, most of the doors were locked to keep people without tickets out, so many members of the audience couldn't escape. The single staircase limited the number of people who could escape from the balcony, and the fire escapes didn't have ladders to climb down.

By the time the fire was extinguished, more than 600 people had died. After the fire, the bodies of those who died were placed in the alley behind the theater, earning it the nickname Death Alley. Since then, people passing through the alley have reported hearing weak cries, seeing ghosts, and feeling as though they were being touched or pushed when no one else was around.

Although the theater was torn down and the James M. Nederlander Theatre now stands in its place, there are still reports of paranormal occurrences. One night, while on a break at the theater, a stage manager was having a cigarette outside when he heard a voice say, "Smoke will kill you." When he looked up, he saw a woman in a hoop skirt and a big hat standing beside him. Then she disappeared from sight. On another evening, after everyone had left for the night, a stagehand heard a toilet flush in the women's bathroom and the sound of young girls giggling. When he entered the bathroom, nobody was there.

WHAT CHANGED AFTER THE FIRE?

In the months and years after the Iroquois Theatre fire, many changes were made to fire regulations to prevent a disaster like that fire from happening again, and the rules were more strictly enforced. Changes included push bars called panic bars that allow people to push the door open even while it is locked from the other side. Doors also had to open outward so people could get out quickly, and sprinkler systems and emergency lighting became normal fixtures in buildings.

CHICAGO
HAUNTED SPOTS

Chicago has a very dark and violent history. There are many supposedly haunted locations found throughout the city. Sites vary in age, history, and location. What types of locations are reported to be haunted? Which sites mentioned in the book are you most curious about? How does the map help you understand these locations?

SCIENCE OF GHOSTS

There are many scientific and psychological factors that can explain why people believe in ghosts and hauntings. Infrasound is a low-frequency sound just below the range of what humans can hear. It is common in buildings and can be created by human-made objects such as air conditioners, air circulators, or road traffic. Infrasound can also be created naturally by storms, wind, and other weather patterns.

People may respond to infrasound subconsciously with feelings of fear, anxiety, or extreme sadness. They may also experience

People who hunt for ghosts may use technology to detect things such as infrasound.

Floors or door hinges in old buildings, such as historic hotels, might creak or make other noises. These can also create a creepy feeling.

the chills. Some scientists think that supposedly haunted sites have a level of infrasound that may cause people to have strange feelings that they connect to ghosts.

The human mind is very open to suggestion. Studies show that if a person is told a location is haunted, they will report more cold spots or changes in temperature compared with a person who isn't told that a place is haunted. Hearing ghost stories and watching scary movies also make people more open to the idea that ghosts are real. This is a possible explanation for why so many people claim to have seen or felt something supernatural.

Additionally, human brains have something called agency detection mechanisms. These help protect people from harm. When people don't have enough information to properly understand something, their brains create stories to explain what's going on. Psychologists believe that these mechanisms can explain why people believe in ghosts and hauntings.

STONE TAPE THEORY

Many structures in Chicago. such as the Chicago Water Tower, are built from limestone. According to some paranormal investigators, limestone can hang on to energy from the past and replay it like a movie. This idea is called the stone tape theory of residual haunting, named for a 1970s British TV movie called *The Stone Tape*. The film made this theory popular.

For example, when the guards at the Cook County Jail couldn't find a reason for the strange noises and occurrences, they may have decided that they were caused by paranormal activity.

GHOST HUNTING

However, some insist that people truly are experiencing the paranormal in at least some situations. People have been trying to communicate with ghosts and prove their existence for many centuries. Modern ghost hunters use many tools to try to find ghosts.

One of the most important tools is a digital voice recorder that detects electronic voice phenomena (EVP). EVP are the unexplained sounds and voices on electronic devices. The people who investigate ghost activity believe that these recordings are the voices of spirits trying to communicate with the living. Some experts suggest that since spirits can't properly talk, they use their energy to electronically arrange sound into something that sounds like a voice.

BELIEF IN THE
PARANORMAL

PERSONALLY ENCOUNTERED A GHOST

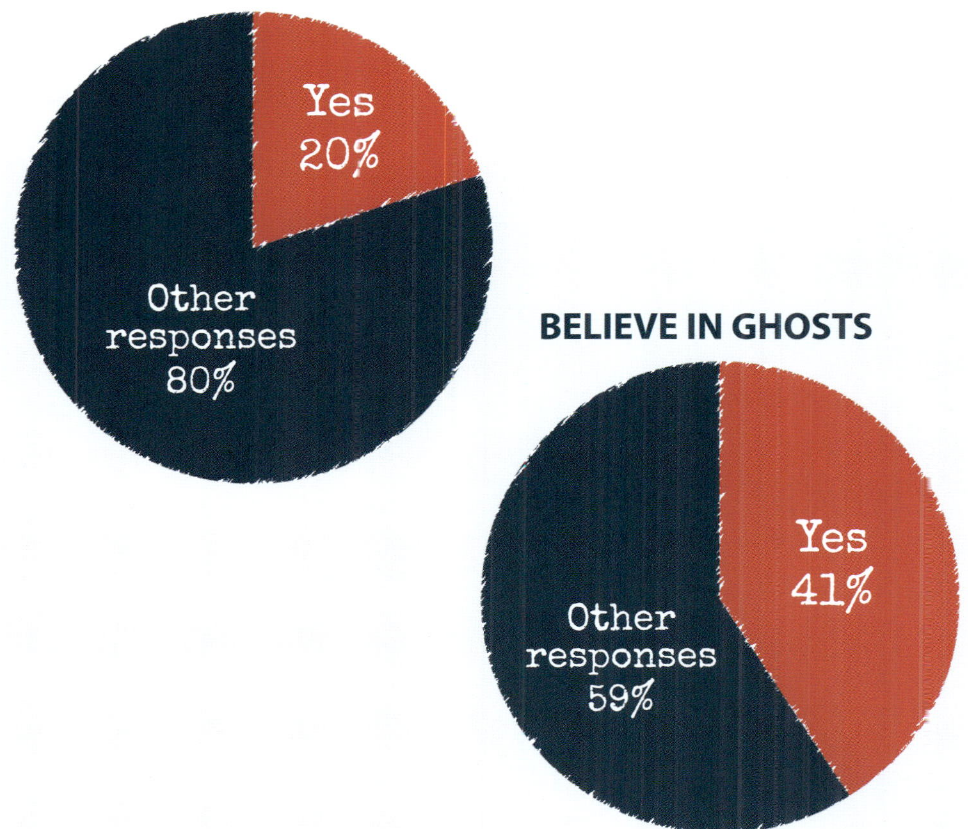

PERSPECTIVES

GHOSTLY PROOF

Many people who try to prove or disprove that ghosts exist believe that science will give them the answers, but this is easier said than done. Elaine, a ghost tour guide in New Orleans, says:

> *The paranormal is, by its nature, almost impossible scientifically [to] prove. For something to be scientifically provable, it must be capable of being disproved with experiments that can be repeated. You never know if a ghost is going to show up, if it is going to be able to give you evidence, or if it will be the same evidence as last week.*

Another tool that's used is a full spectrum camera. These cameras are used in dark or low-light environments because that's where ghost hunters believe they will see the most paranormal activity. People often think that ghosts are manipulating light so they can't be seen with the naked eye. Full spectrum cameras capture images that might be visible only in infrared or ultraviolet light. Most ghost hunters will also carry an electromagnetic field (EMF) detector.

An electromagnetic field is the combination of invisible electric and magnetic forces. They are created by natural events such as Earth's magnetic field or by human actions such as the use of electricity.

Paranormal researchers and ghost hunters believe ghosts can produce electromagnetic fields. They say ghosts use them to cause mysterious events such as flickering lights and doors opening and closing on their own. Many supposedly haunted locations have strong magnetic fields. However, according to scientific research, EMFs can also affect some parts of the brain that will make a person think that someone, such as a ghost, is in the room with them.

There are many scientific and psychological explanations for why some people believe that ghosts are real. At the same time, there are many paranormal occurrences that science and reason haven't yet explained. So people will continue to visit Chicago and its haunted locations in hopes of personally witnessing paranormal activity.

FAST FACTS

- Chicago's violent history has helped give it a reputation as being one of the most haunted cities in the United States.

- The Congress Plaza Hotel is reported to be one of the most haunted spots in the state of Illinois.

- The Chicago Water Tower was one of the few structures that didn't burn down in the Great Chicago Fire of 1871.

- The hangings at the old Cook County Jail have led to reports of hauntings at the site, which is now a fire station.

- More than 100 hauntings have been reported at Bachelor's Grove Cemetery.

- Resurrection Mary is one of Chicago's most famous ghosts. People generally claim to spot her near Resurrection Cemetery.

- The ghost of the famous bank robber John Dillinger is said to haunt the site of the Biograph Theater.

- The ghosts of people who died in the Iroquois Theatre fire are said to still haunt the site.

- Psychological factors can explain why some people believe in ghosts.

- Ghost hunters use a variety of tools to try to prove that ghosts exist.

You Are There

This book discusses hauntings in Chicago, Illinois. Imagine you are looking for ghosts in Chicago. Write a letter home telling your friends what you have found. What places do you visit? Be sure to add plenty of detail in your notes.

Dig Deeper

After reading this book, what questions do you still have about the many ghosts who haunt the Red Lion Pub? With an adult's help, find a few reliable sources that can help you answer your questions. Write a paragraph about what you learned.

Tell the Tale

Chapter Three discusses some of the supernatural occurrences at Bachelor's Grove Cemetery. Imagine you are walking through the cemetery. Write 200 words about the strange things you might experience there. How would you try to explain to someone else what you saw?

Another View

This book discusses some of the reasons why people might believe in ghosts and hauntings. As you know, every source is different. Ask a librarian or another adult to help you find a second source about the reasons for hauntings. Write a short essay comparing and contrasting the new source's point of view with that of this book's author. What is the point of view of each author? How are they similar and why? How are they different and why?

GLOSSARY

hitchhiker
someone who travels by getting a free ride in another person's car

menacing
threatening

morgue
a place, often in a hospital, where bodies are kept

paranormal
events that can't be explained by science

parapsychologist
a person who studies mental occurrences that can't be explained by psychology

psychological
having to do with the mind or emotions

refugee
a person who is forced to leave his or her home and find protection in another country

subconscious
the part of the mind that affects a person's thoughts and feelings without them realizing it

ONLINE RESOURCES

To learn more about hauntings and Chicago, Illinois, visit our free resource websites below.

Visit **abdocorelibrary.com** or scan this QR code for free Common Core resources for teachers and students, including vetted activities, multimedia, and booklinks, for deeper subject comprehension.

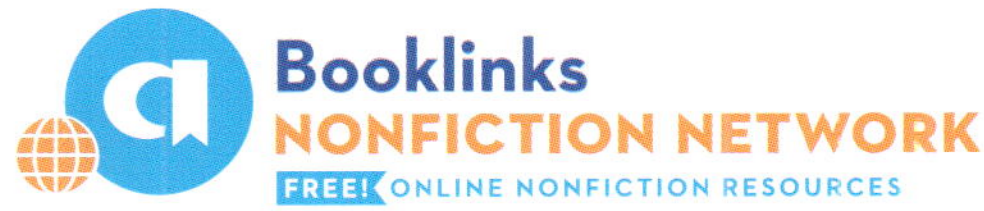

Visit **abdobooklinks.com** or scan this QR code for free additional online weblinks for further learning. These links are routinely monitored and updated to provide the most current information available.

LEARN MORE

Hollihan, Kerrie Logan. *Ghosts Unveiled!* Abrams, 2020.

Shulman, Mark. *Super Cities! Chicago.* Arcadia Children's Books, 2021.

INDEX

About the Author

Rachel is an avid book enthusiast with more than 15 years of experience working with schools and libraries matching books to readers. She is also the author of several nonfiction books for children. When she isn't writing or researching fun facts, she enjoys spending time with her boyfriend and her mischievous dog.